The Best Loved Adventure Of

SHERLOCK HOLMES

THE SPECKLED BAND

By Sir Arthur Conan Doyle

Other Publications

Sherlock Holmes and the Cryptic Clues, McClure, Michael W., Baskerville Productions, Chester, IL, 2016.

The Baker Street News, McClure, Michael W. (editor). Journal of the Chester Baskerville Society, Chester, IL, 1994.

Stimson & Company Gazette, McClure, Michael W. (editor). Journal of Stimson & Company, Chester, IL, Since 1990.

Holmes For The Holidays, McClure, Michael W. (editor). First Sherlockian publication seasonally published for kids of all ages, Cartwright's Companions, Chester, IL, Since 1989.

The Devonshire Chronicle, McClure, Michael W. (editor). Flagship journal of the Chester Baskerville Society, Chester, IL, Since 1988.

Popeye and Friends Character Trail Handbook, McClure, Michael W., Baskerville Productions, Chester, IL, 2021.

Recovery, McClure, Michael W. (editor). Aftercare grief counseling publication, Schroeder-McClure Funeral Home, Chester, IL, 1996.

The Best Loved Adventure Of

SHERLOCK HOLMES

THE SPECKLED BAND

By Sir Arthur Conan Doyle

Edited, With Annotations by

Michael W. McClure

Illustrations by

Tijana Tumbas and Sidney Paget

BASKERVILLE PRODUCTIONS

CHESTER, ILLINOIS

February 2017

The Best Loved Adventure Of
Sherlock Holmes
THE SPECKLED BAND

Published by
Baskerville Productions
1415 Swanwick St.
Chester, IL 62233 USA
www.baskervilleproductions.com

ISBN: 978-0-9981084-2-1

(Original 2017 Black & White Edition is available as
ISBN: 978-0-9981084-3-8)

Published in the United States of America
by permission of Conan Doyle Estate, Ltd.

Colorized, Revised Edition
2021

My love
to
Ellie Marie
&
Catherine Gail
&
Isla Joy
&
My Scions
That Will
Follow.

I Don't Intend
To Spoil Them,
But I Will Be Very
Accommodating!

"Pray be precise as to details."
Sherlock Holmes
"The Speckled Band"

INTRODUCTION

By Michael W. McClure

Which star in the heavens is the most beautiful? All give the same quality of light, but together they offer a magnificent display. Such is the literary universe that was created by a young doctor named Arthur. Each of his recorded adventures of the brilliant investigator, Sherlock Holmes, pulls the reader steadily into a captivating orbit ... just as gravity is a force not to be denied. Since the birth of this stellar sleuth in the 1887 issue of *Beeton's Christmas Annual,* millions of devoted mystery lovers around the world have been captured by the allure of a master storyteller.

1859 heralded the birth of Arthur Conan Doyle in Scotland's capital city, Edinburgh. His pursuit of a medical degree brought him into contact with an inspiring, trailblazing professor. Conan Doyle would never forget his favorite teacher, Dr. Joseph Bell, and the analytical methods he pioneered. Bell's astute powers of deduction and observation were mirrored by Conan Doyle in Sherlock and useful in his unique profession ... the world's first consulting detective.

Conan Doyle penned a total of sixty different adventures that involved Sherlock Holmes and his faithful friend and assistant, Dr. John H. Watson. The duo took up a London residence in Mrs. Hudson's second floor suite of rooms located at 221 Baker Street, now one of the most famous addresses in the world. They solved crimes and helped many people during their storied careers, which spanned the reigns of Queen Victoria, King Edward VI and King George V. The Grand Sherlockian Game, that this annotated volume continues, is to postulate that Holmes and Watson really exist ... after all, they never died!

Of the fifty-six short stories, which tale deserves the title of favorite? Which narrative consistently shines the brightest? Several official surveys (see page 72) have been taken over the last century, and *The Adventure of the Speckled Band* has always risen to the top, but we defer to an even more discerning intellect for our final designation. The author of this wonderful world of imagination, Sir Arthur Conan Doyle, when asked in 1927 to name his favorite short story, wrote that he selected "the grim story of '*The Speckled Band*', that I am sure will be on every list!"

And now his favorite adventure begins ....

Illustration of Sir Arthur Conan Doyle
By Anna Sushchenko

THE SPECKLED BAND

BAND

By Sir Arthur Conan Doyle

In glancing over my notes of the seventy odd cases in which *I have during the last eight years*

studied the methods of my friend Sherlock Holmes,[1] I find many tragic, some comic, a large number merely strange, but none commonplace; for, working as he did rather for the love of his art than for the acquirement of wealth, he refused to associate himself with any investigation which did not tend towards the unusual, and even the fantastic. Of all these varied cases, however, I cannot recall any which presented more *singular*[2] features than that which was associated with the well-known *Surrey*[3] family of the *Roylotts of Stoke Moran.*[4] The events in question occurred in the early days of my association with Holmes, when we were sharing rooms as bachelors, in *Baker Street.*[5] It is possible that I might have placed

---

[1] Since Sherlock Holmes and Dr. Watson met in 1881 during "A Study In Scarlet", eight years for observation indicates that this adventure was recalled and written by Watson in 1889. It was not published until February 1892. It is important to note that Dr. Watson did not accompany Holmes on all of his cases.

[2] Here singular means "out of the ordinary" features.

[3] Surrey is a county in the southeast of England and referred to as one of the home counties bordering Greater London.

[4] The Roylott name is not found to be of historical importance, so it must have been substituted by Dr. Watson in order to disguise the real family name attached to this adventure. The name did remind Sir Arthur Conan Doyle in 1921 of an excellent cricket bowler named Arnold Rylott. There is a village named Stoke D'Abernon in the appropriate area of this tale, but the name, Moran, is an Irish surname (last name) of an old respected family.

[5] Baker Street is in the City of Westminster, London, England, where Sherlock Holmes and, occasionally, Dr. Watson lived.

them upon record before, but a promise of secrecy was made at the time, from which I have only been freed during the last month by the *untimely death of the lady* [6] to whom the pledge was given. It is perhaps as well that the facts should now come to light, for I have reasons to know there are widespread rumours as to the death of Dr. Grimesby Roylott which tend to make the matter even more terrible than the truth.

It was early in April in the *year '83* [7] that I woke one morning to find Sherlock Holmes standing, fully dressed, by the side of my bed. He was a late riser as a rule, and, as the clock on the mantelpiece showed me that it was only a *quarter-past seven,* [8] I blinked up at him in some surprise, and perhaps just a little resentment, for I was myself regular in my habits.

"Very sorry to *knock you up,* [9] Watson," said he, "but it's the common lot this morning. Mrs. Hudson has been knocked up, she *retorted* [10] upon me, and I on you."

"What is it, then? A fire?"

---

[6] Undoubtedly the untimely death of his soon-to-be client, Miss Helen Stoner, in only five short years after the adventure occurred.

[7] 1883

[8] One quarter of an hour, or fifteen minutes, after seven in the morning.

[9] British phrase meaning "to awaken as by knocking at the door".

[10] Responded, sharply, with same action to another person.

"No, a client. It seems that a young lady has arrived in a considerable state of excitement, who insists upon seeing me. She is waiting now in the *sitting-room* [11]. Now, when young ladies wander about the *metropolis* [12] at this hour of the morning and knock sleepy people up out of their beds, I presume that it is something very pressing which they have to communicate. Should it prove to be an interesting case, you would, I am sure, wish to follow it from the outset. I thought at any rate that I should call you, and give you the chance."

"My dear fellow, I would not miss it for anything."

I had no keener pleasure than in following Holmes in his professional investigations, and in admiring the rapid deductions, as swift as intuitions, and yet always founded on a logical basis, with which he unraveled the problems which were submitted to him. I rapidly threw on my clothes, and was ready in a few minutes to accompany my friend down to the sitting-room. A lady dressed in black and heavily veiled, who had been sitting in the window, rose as we entered.

"Good morning, madam," said Holmes, cheerily. "My name is Sherlock Holmes. This is my intimate friend and associate, Dr. Watson, before whom you can speak as freely as before

[11] A small, comfortable room where people can sit and talk.
[12] The capital or chief city in a country. London's population at this time was just short of six million residents.

myself. Ha, I am glad to see that Mrs. Hudson has
had the good sense to light the fire. Pray draw up

to it, and I shall *order you a cup of hot coffee,*[13] for I observe that you are shivering."

"It is not cold which makes me shiver," said the woman in a low voice, changing her seat as requested.

"What then?"

"It is fear, Mr. Holmes. It is terror." She raised her veil as she spoke, and we could see that she was indeed in a pitiable state of agitation, her face all drawn and gray, with restless, frightened eyes, like those of some hunted animal. Her features and figure were those of a woman of thirty, but her hair was shot with premature gray, and her expression was weary and haggard.

Sherlock Holmes ran her over with one of his quick, all-comprehensive glances.

"You must not fear," said he, soothingly, bending forward and patting her forearm. "We shall soon set matters right, I have no doubt. You have come in by train this morning, I see."

"You know me, then?"

"No, but I observe the second half of a return ticket in the palm of your left glove. You must have started early, and yet you had a good drive in

---

[13] Since Starbucks and other coffee houses did not exist at this time, Mrs. Hudson, Holmes' landlady, provided the food and drinks for both of her lodgers and their guests.

a *dogcart,*[14] along heavy roads, before you reached the station."

The lady gave a violent start, and stared in bewilderment at my companion.

"There is no mystery, my dear madam," said he, smiling. "The left arm of your jacket is spattered with mud in no less than seven places. The marks are perfectly fresh. There is no vehicle save a dog-cart which throws up mud in that way, and then only when you sit on the left-hand side of the driver."

"Whatever your reasons may be, you are perfectly correct," said she. "I started from home before six, reached *Leatherhead*[15] at twenty past, and came in by the first train to *Waterloo.*[16] Sir, I can stand this strain no longer, I shall go mad if it continues. I have no one to turn to - none, save only one, who cares for me, and he, poor fellow, can be of little aid. I have heard of you, Mr. Holmes; I have heard of you from *Mrs. Farintosh,*[17] whom you helped in the hour of her sore need. It was from her that I had your address. Oh, sir, do you not think that you could

---

[14] A two wheeled horse drawn vehicle.

[15] A small town on the river Mole, Leatherhead lies about eighteen miles southwest of London.

[16] The Waterloo Train Station was built in 1848 and was a major railway connection.

[17] An example of one of many cases Dr. Watson hinted at, but never released to the reading public. At least we know this case concerned an opal tiara ... a jeweled band worn on the front of a woman's hair.

help me too, and at least throw a little light through the dense darkness which surrounds me? At present it is out of my power to reward you for your services, but in a month or six weeks I shall be married, with the control of my own income, and then at least you shall not find me ungrateful."

Holmes turned to his desk, and unlocking it, drew out a small case-book which he consulted.

"Farintosh," said he. "Ah, yes, I recall the case; it was concerned with an opal tiara. I think it was before your time, Watson. I can only say, madam, that I shall be happy to devote the same care to your case as I did to that of your friend. As to reward, my profession is its own reward; but you are at liberty to defray whatever expenses I may be put to, at the time which suits you best. And now I beg that you will lay before us everything that may help us in forming an opinion upon the matter."

"Alas!" replied our visitor. "The very horror of my situation lies in the fact that my fears are so vague, and my suspicions depend so entirely upon small points, which might seem trivial to another, that even he to whom of all others I have a right to look for help and advice looks upon all that I tell him about it as the fancies of a nervous woman. He does not say so, but I can read it from his soothing answers and averted eyes. But I have heard, Mr. Holmes, that you can see deeply into the *manifold* [18] wickedness of the human heart. You may advise me how to walk amid the dangers which encompass me."

"I am all attention, madam."

"My name is Helen Stoner, and I am living with my stepfather, who is the last survivor of one of the oldest *Saxon families in England,* [19] the Roylotts of Stoke Moran, on the western border of Surrey." Holmes nodded his head.

"The name is familiar to me," said he.

"The family was at one time among the richest in England, and the estate extended over the borders into *Berkshire* [20] in the north, and *Hampshire* [21] in the west. In the last century, however, four successive heirs were of a dissolute and wasteful disposition, and the family ruin was eventually completed by a gambler, in the days of the *Regency.* [22] Nothing was left save a few acres of ground and the two-hundred-year-old house, which is itself crushed under a heavy mortgage. The last *squire* [23] dragged out his existence there,

---

[18] Many or of great variety

[19] The Anglo-Saxons were a Germanic people that settled in Britain during the 5th century .

[20] A county in South East England that lies to the west of London.

[21] The largest county in South East England.

[22] A period of time from 1811 to 1820 during which King George III's insanity made him unfit to rule. His son, the Prince of Wales, ruled in his stead. The Prince later became King George IV.

[23] A well-respected man; usually the largest land owner in the area.

living the horrible life of an *aristocratic pauper,*[24] but his only son, my stepfather, seeing that he must adapt himself to the new conditions,

STOKE MORAN

[24] A person who is noble by birth, but lacks the money to maintain the expensive quality of living that is expected from a high ranking individual in society.

obtained an advance from a relative, which enabled him to take a medical degree, and went out to *Calcutta*,[25] where, by his professional skill and his force of character, he established a large practice. In a fit of anger, however, caused by some robberies which had been perpetrated in the house, he beat his native butler to death, and narrowly escaped a *capital sentence*.[26] As it was, he suffered a long term of imprisonment, and afterwards returned to England a *morose*[27] and disappointed man.

"When Dr. Roylott was in India he married my mother, Mrs. Stoner, the young widow of Major-General Stoner, of the *Bengal Artillery*.[28] My sister Julia and I were twins, and we were only two years old at the time of my mother's remarriage. She had a considerable sum of money, not less than a *thousand a year*,[29] and this she bequeathed to Dr. Roylott entirely whilst we resided with him, with a provision that a certain annual sum should be allowed to each of us in the event of our marriage. Shortly after our return to England my mother died - she was killed eight years ago in *a railway*

---

[25] The Victorian era spelling of "Kolkata" when it was the capital of British India.

[26] The lawful use of death as a punishment.

[27] Bad tempered and depressed

[28] An army in India under the direct authority of the British Crown.

[29] The annual value of 1000 British pounds in 1883 is worth 109,000 pounds in 2016, which is the equivalent to over $156,000 US.

accident near Crewe.[30] Dr. Roylott then abandoned his attempts to establish himself in practice in London, and took us to live with him in the ancestral house at Stoke Moran. The money which my mother had left was enough for all our wants, and there seemed no obstacle to our happiness.

"But a terrible change came over our stepfather about this time. Instead of making friends and exchanging visits with our neighbours, who had at first been overjoyed to see a Roylott of Stoke Moran back in the old family seat, he shut himself up in his house and seldom came out save to indulge in ferocious quarrels with whoever might cross his path. Violence of temper approaching to mania has been hereditary in the men of the family, and in my stepfather's case it had, I believe, been intensified by his long residence in the tropics. A series of disgraceful brawls took place, two of which ended in the police-court, until at last he became the terror of the village, and the folks would fly at his approach, for he is a man of immense strength, and absolutely uncontrollable in his anger.

"Last week he hurled the local blacksmith over a *parapet*[31] into a stream, and it was only by paying

---

[30] In this Cheshire railway town, located in the north-west of England, there was an accident on Nov. 13, 1874, undoubtedly the one that claimed the twins' mother.

[31] In this case, a low wall on the side of a bridge.

over all the money that I could gather together that I was able to avert another public exposure. He had no friends at all save the wandering *gipsies,*[32] and he would give these *vagabonds* [33] leave to encamp upon the few acres of bramble-covered land which represent the family estate, and would accept in return the hospitality of their tents, wandering away with them sometimes for weeks on end. He has a passion also for Indian animals, which are sent over to him by a *correspondent,*[34] and he has at this moment a cheetah and a baboon, which wander freely over his grounds, and are feared by the villagers almost as much as their master.

"You can imagine from what I say that my poor sister Julia and I had no great pleasure in our lives. No servant would stay with us, and for a long time we did all the work of the house. She was but thirty at the time of her death, and yet her hair had already begun to whiten, even as mine has."

"Your sister is dead, then?"

"She died just two years ago, and it is of her death that I wish to speak to you. You can understand that, living the life which I have described, we were little likely to see anyone of

---

[32] Conan Doyle's term indicating a group of traveling people, also known as the Romani, that are believed to have originated in South Asia.

[33] People who wander about without a home or job.

[34] A person or agency in a remote place that transacts business on behalf of another.

our own age and position. We had, however, an aunt, my mother's *maiden*[35] sister, Miss Honoria Westphail, who lives near *Harrow,*[36] and we were occasionally allowed to pay short visits at this lady's house. Julia went there at Christmas two years ago, and met there a *half-pay Major of Marines,*[37] to whom she became engaged. My stepfather learned of the engagement when my sister returned, and offered no objection to the marriage; but within a *fortnight*[38] of the day which had been fixed for the wedding, the terrible event occurred which has deprived me of my only companion."

Sherlock Holmes had been leaning back in his chair with his eyes closed, and his head sunk in a cushion, but he half opened his lids now, and glanced across at his visitor.

"Pray be precise as to details," said he.

"It is easy for me to be so, for every event of that dreadful time is seared into my memory. The manor house is, as I have already said, very old, and only one wing is now inhabited. The bedrooms in this wing are on the ground floor, the sitting-rooms being in the central block of the buildings. Of these bedrooms, the first is Dr.

---

[35] An unmarried female.

[36] A large suburban town to the northwest of London.

[37] Half-pay was a reduced wage for soldiers that were not on active duty, but could be called back to action at any time; a Major was an officer of mid-level command status.

[38] A period of two weeks.

Roylott's, the second my sister's, and the third my own. There is no communication between them, but they all open out into the same corridor. Do I make myself plain?"

"Perfectly so."

"The windows of the three rooms open out upon the lawn. That fatal night Dr. Roylott had gone to his room early, though we knew that he had not retired to rest, for my sister was troubled by the smell of the strong Indian cigars which it was his custom to smoke. She left her room, therefore, and came into mine, where she sat for some time, chatting about her approaching wedding. At eleven o'clock she rose to leave me, but she paused at the door and looked back.

" 'Tell me, Helen,' said she, `have you ever heard anyone whistle in the dead of the night?'

" 'Never,' said I.

" 'I suppose that you could not possibly whistle, yourself, in your sleep?'

" 'Certainly not. But why?'

" 'Because during the last few nights I have always, about three in the morning, heard a low clear whistle. I am a light sleeper, and it has awakened me. I cannot tell where it came from - perhaps from the next room, perhaps from the lawn. I thought that I would just ask you whether you had heard it.'

" 'No, I have not. It must be those wretched gipsies in the plantation.'

" 'Very likely. And yet if it were on the lawn I wonder that you did not hear it also.'

" 'Ah, but I sleep more heavily than you.'

" 'Well, it is of no great consequence, at any rate,' she smiled back at me, closed my door, and a few moments later I heard her key turn in the lock."

"Indeed," said Holmes. "Was it your custom always to lock yourselves in at night?"

"Always."

"And why?"

"I think that I mentioned to you that the Doctor kept a cheetah and a baboon. We had no feeling of security unless our doors were locked."

"Quite so. Pray proceed with your statement."

"I could not sleep that night. A vague feeling of impending misfortune impressed me. My sister and I, you will recollect, were twins, and you know how subtle are the links which bind two souls which are so closely allied. It was a wild night. The wind was howling outside, and the rain was beating and splashing against the windows. Suddenly, amidst all the hubbub of the gale, there burst forth the wild scream of a terrified woman. I knew that it was my sister's voice. I sprang from my bed, wrapped a shawl round me, and rushed into the corridor. As I opened my door I seemed to hear a low whistle, such as my sister described, and a few moments later a clanging sound, as if a mass of metal had fallen. As I ran down the passage my sister's door was unlocked, and revolved slowly upon its hinges. I stared at it horror-stricken, not knowing what was about to issue from it. By the light of the corridor lamp I saw my sister appear at the opening, her face *blanched* [39] with terror, her hands groping for help, her whole figure swaying to and fro like that of a drunkard. I ran to her and threw my arms round her, but at that moment her knees seemed to give way and she fell to the ground. She writhed as one who is in terrible pain, and her limbs were dreadfully convulsed. At first I thought that she had not recognized me, but as I bent over her she suddenly shrieked out in a voice which I shall never forget, 'Oh, my God! Helen! It was the band! The speckled band!' There was something else which she would *fain* [40] have said, and she stabbed with her finger into the air in the direction of the Doctor's room, but a fresh convulsion seized her and choked her words. I rushed out, calling loudly for my stepfather, and I met him hastening from his room in his dressing-gown. When he reached my sister's side she was unconscious, and though he *poured brandy down*

---

[39] Grew pale from shock or fear.
[40] An old fashioned word meaning she eagerly wanted to say something more.

her throat,[41] and sent for medical aid from the village, all efforts were in vain, for she slowly sank and died without having recovered her consciousness. Such was the dreadful end of my beloved sister."

"One moment," said Holmes; "are you sure about this whistle and metallic sound? Could you swear to it?"

"That was what the *county coroner asked me at the inquiry.*[42] It is my strong impression that I heard it, and yet among the crash of the gale, and the creaking of an old house, I may possibly have been deceived."

"Was your sister dressed?"

"No, she was in her nightdress. In her right hand was found the charred stump of a match, and in her left a matchbox."

"Showing that she had struck a light and looked about her when the alarm took place. That is important. And what conclusions did the coroner come to?"

"He investigated the case with great care, for Dr. Roylott's conduct had long been notorious in the county, but he was unable to find any satisfactory

---

[41] In the Victorian era, this alcoholic drink was thought to have widespread medical benefits. Dr. Watson offered brandy often to his patients in case of emergencies.

[42] It was the Coroner's duty to investigate the cause of unnatural deaths and report this at a juried inquest or simple inquiry.

cause of death. My evidence showed that the door had been fastened upon the inner side, and the windows were blocked by old-fashioned shutters with broad iron bars, which were secured every night. The walls were carefully *sounded,*[43] and were shown to be quite solid all round, and the flooring was also thoroughly examined, with the same result. The chimney is wide, but is *barred up by four large staples.*[44] It is certain, therefore, that my sister was quite alone when she met her end. Besides, there were no marks of any violence upon her."

"How about poison?"

"The doctors examined her for it, but without success."

"What do you think that this unfortunate lady died of, then?"

"It is my belief that she died of pure fear and nervous shock, though what it was which frightened her I cannot imagine."

"Were there gipsies in the plantation at the time?"

"Yes, there are nearly always some there."

"Ah, and what did you gather from this allusion to a band - a speckled band?"

---

[43] Examined by beating upon a surface to detect hollowness.
[44] Metal bars installed inside the chimney to prevent anyone from climbing down the shaft and entering the house uninvited.

"Sometimes I have thought that it was merely the wild talk of *delirium*,[45] sometimes that it may have referred to some band of people, perhaps to these very gipsies in the plantation. I do not know whether the spotted handkerchiefs which so many of them wear over their heads might have suggested the strange adjective which she used."

Holmes shook his head like a man who is far from being satisfied.

"These are very *deep waters*,[46]" said he; "pray go on with your narrative."

"Two years have passed since then, and my life has been until lately lonelier than ever. A month ago, however, a dear friend, whom I have known for many years, has done me the honour to ask my hand in marriage. His name is Armitage - Percy Armitage - the second son of Mr. Armitage, of *Crane Water, near Reading*.[47] My stepfather has offered no opposition to the match, and we are to be married in the course of the spring. Two days ago some repairs were started in the west wing of the building, and my bedroom wall has been pierced, so that I have had to move into the chamber in which my sister died, and to sleep in the very bed in which she slept. Imagine, then, my

---

[45] Confused thinking and reduced awareness of surroundings.
[46] A difficult situation or puzzle.
[47] Crane Water is a fictional location in Reading (pronounced Red-ding), a large town 36 miles west of London.

24

thrill of terror when last night, as I lay awake, thinking over her terrible fate, I suddenly heard in the silence of the night the low whistle which had been the herald of her own death. I sprang up and lit the lamp, but nothing was to be seen in the room. I was too shaken to go to bed again, however, so I dressed, and as soon as it was daylight I slipped down, got a dogcart at the Crown Inn, which is opposite, and drove to Leatherhead, from whence I have come on this morning, with the one object of seeing you and asking your advice."

"You have done wisely," said my friend. "But have you told me all?"

"Yes, all."

"Miss Stoner, you have not. You are screening your stepfather.

"Why, what do you mean?"

For answer Holmes pushed back the frill of black lace which fringed the hand that lay upon our visitor's knee. Five little livid spots, the marks of four fingers and a thumb, were printed upon the white wrist.

"You have been cruelly used," said Holmes.

The lady *coloured deeply*,[48] and covered over her injured wrist. "He is a hard man," she said, "and perhaps he hardly knows his own strength."

---

[48] She blushed, which added color to her face and especially the cheeks.

There was a long silence, during which Holmes
leaned his chin upon his hands and stared into the
crackling fire.

"This is a very deep business," he said at last. "There are a thousand details which I should desire to know before I decide upon our course of action. Yet we have not a moment to lose. If we were to come to Stoke Moran today, would it be possible for us to see over these rooms without the knowledge of your stepfather?"

"As it happens, he spoke of coming into town today upon some most important business. It is probable that he will be away all day, and that there would be nothing to disturb you. We have a housekeeper now, but she is old and foolish, and I could easily get her out of the way."

"Excellent. You are not averse to this trip, Watson?"

"By no means."

"Then we shall both come. What are you going to do yourself?"

"I have one or two things which I would wish to do now that I am in town. But I shall return by the twelve o'clock train, so as to be there in time for your coming."

"And you may expect us early in the afternoon. I have myself some small business matters to attend to. Will you not wait and breakfast?"

"No, I must go. My heart is lightened already since I have confided my trouble to you. I shall look forward to seeing you again this afternoon." She dropped her thick black veil over her face, and glided from the room.

"And what do you think of it all, Watson?" asked Sherlock Holmes, leaning back in his chair.

"It seems to me to be a most dark and sinister business."

"Dark enough and sinister enough."

"Yet if the lady is correct in saying that the flooring and walls are sound, and that the door, window, and chimney are impassable, then her sister must have been undoubtedly alone when she met her mysterious end."

"What becomes, then, of these nocturnal whistles, and what of the very peculiar words of the dying woman?"

"I cannot think."

"When you combine the ideas of whistles at night, the presence of a band of gipsies who are on intimate terms with this old doctor, the fact that we have every reason to believe that the doctor has an interest in preventing his stepdaughter's marriage, the dying allusion to a band, and, finally, the fact that Miss Helen Stoner heard a metallic clang, which might have been caused by one of those metal bars which secured the shutters falling back into their place, I think there is good ground to think that the mystery may be cleared along those lines.

"But what, then, did the gipsies do?"

"I cannot imagine."

"I see many objections to any such a theory."

"And so do I. It is precisely for that reason that we are going to Stoke Moran this day. I want to see whether the objections are fatal, or if they may be explained away. But what, in the name of the devil!"

The ejaculation had been drawn from my companion by the fact that our door had been suddenly dashed open, and that a huge man framed himself in the aperture. His costume was a peculiar mixture of the professional and of the agricultural, having a black top-hat, a long frock-coat, and a pair of *high gaiters,*[49] with a *hunting-crop* [50] swinging in his hand. So tall was he that his hat actually brushed the crossbar of the doorway, and his breadth seemed to span it across from side to side. A large face, seared with a thousand wrinkles, burned yellow with the sun, and marked with every evil passion, was turned from one to the other of us, while his deep-set, *bile-shot* [51]eyes, and the high thin fleshless nose, gave him somewhat the resemblance to a fierce old bird of prey.

"Which of you is Holmes?" asked this apparition.

"My name, sir, but you have the advantage of me," said my companion, quietly.

---

[49] A garment worn to protect the ankle and lower leg.
[50] A short type of whip used in horse riding.
[51] Sickly yellow or slightly greenish.

"I am Dr. Grimesby Roylott, of Stoke Moran."

"Indeed. Doctor," said Holmes, blandly. "Pray take a seat."

"I will do nothing of the kind. My stepdaughter has been here. I have traced her. What has she been saying to you?"

"It is a little cold for the time of the year," said Holmes.

"What has she been saying to you?" screamed the old man furiously.

"But I have heard that the *crocuses* [52] promise well,"
continued my companion *imperturbably*. [53]

"Ha! You put me off, do you?" said our new visitor, taking a step forward, and shaking his hunting-crop. "I know you, you scoundrel! I have heard of you before. You are Holmes the meddler."

My friend smiled.

"Holmes the busybody!"

His smile broadened.

"Holmes the Scotland Yard *jack-in-office*. [54]"

Holmes chuckled heartily. "Your conversation is most entertaining," said he. "When you go out close the door, for there is a decided *draught*. [55]"

---

[52] Flowering plant in the iris family.

[53] Calmly and not able to be excited.

[54] Roylott referred to Holmes as a self-important minor official and used the same term to insult him when he accused him of working for Scotland Yard. Holmes was an independent consulting detective and not subject to any higher authority.

[55] Noticeable current of wind or draft.

"I will go when I have had my say. Don't you dare to meddle with my affairs. I know that Miss Stoner has been here - I traced her! I am a dangerous man to fall foul of! See here." He stepped swiftly forward, seized the *poker,*[56] and bent it into a curve with his huge brown hands.

---

[56] A fireplace tool used to adjust the coal or wood when burning.

"See that you keep yourself out of my grip," he snarled, and hurling the twisted poker into the fireplace, he strode out of the room.

"He seems a very amiable person," said Holmes, laughing. "I am not quite so bulky, but if he had remained I might have shown him that my grip was not much more feeble than his own." As he spoke he picked up the steel poker, and with a sudden effort *straightened it out again.*[57]

"Fancy his having the *insolence to confound me with the official detective force!*[58] This incident gives zest to our investigation, however, and I only trust that our little friend will not suffer from her imprudence in allowing this brute to trace her. And now, Watson, we shall order breakfast, and afterwards I shall walk down to *Doctors' Commons,*[59] where I hope to get some data which may help us in this matter."

It was nearly one o'clock when Sherlock Holmes returned from his excursion. He held in his hand a sheet of blue paper, scrawled over with notes and figures.

---

[57] It took greater strength in the arms and shoulders to straighten a fireplace poker than it did to bend it. Holmes demonstrated his superiority over Roylott for both Watson's and our benefit.

[58] Holmes considered it rude for Roylott to think he worked for Scotland Yard.

[59] The usual name given to the College of Advocates and Doctors of Law. The building was demolished sixteen years before this case, and the Will Office was transferred to Somerset House. Holmes probably used the old nickname here out of habit.

"I have seen the will of the deceased wife," said he. "To determine its exact meaning I have been obliged to work out the present prices of the investments with which it is concerned. The total income, which at the time of the wife's death was little short of £1,100, is now through the fall in agricultural prices not more than £750. Each daughter can claim an income of £250, in case of marriage. It is evident, therefore, that if both girls had married *this beauty would have had a mere pittance,*[60] while even one of them would cripple him to a serious extent. My morning's work has not been wasted, since it has proved that he has the very strongest motives for standing in the way of anything of the sort. And now, Watson, this is too serious for *dawdling,*[61] especially as the old man is aware that we are interesting ourselves in his affairs, so if you are ready we shall call a cab and drive to Waterloo. I should be very much obliged if you would slip your revolver into your pocket. An *Eley's No. 2*[62] is an excellent argument with gentlemen who can twist steel pokers into

---

[60] Roylott's share would have been cut to one third if both daughters took their inheritance, so Holmes felt this would have left too little for Roylott to manage all of the properties' upkeep and repairs. Although his portion would still be worth almost $40,000 in today's United States currency (value in 2017), that would not have been enough to maintain his property and standard of living.

[61] Wasting time or moving too slowly.

[62] Holmes refers to the actual bullet that fit the Webley's No. 2 revolver, a small pocket pistol.

knots. That and a toothbrush are, I think, all that we need."

At Waterloo we were fortunate in catching a train for Leatherhead, where we hired a *trap*[63] at the station inn, and drove for four or five miles through the lovely Surrey lanes. It was a perfect day, with a bright sun and a few fleecy clouds in the heavens. The trees and wayside hedges were just throwing out their first green shoots, and the air was full of the pleasant smell of the moist earth. To me at least there was a strange contrast between the sweet promise of the spring and this sinister quest upon which we were engaged. My companion sat in front of the trap, his arms folded, his hat pulled down over his eyes, and his chin sunk upon his breast, buried in the deepest thought. Suddenly, however, he started, tapped me on the shoulder, and pointed over the meadows.

"Look there!" said he.

A heavily timbered park stretched up in a gentle slope, thickening into a grove at the highest point. From amid the branches there jutted out the gray gables and high roof-tree of a very old mansion.

"Stoke Moran?" said he.

"Yes, sir, that be the house of Dr. Grimesby Roylott," remarked the driver.

---

[63] A small two or four wheeled horse drawn carriage.

"There is some building going on there," said
Holmes; "that is where we are going."

"There's the village," said the driver, pointing to
a cluster of roofs some distance to the left; "but if
you want to get to the house, you'll find it shorter

to go over this *stile*,[64] and so by the footpath over the fields. There it is, where the lady is walking."

"And the lady, I fancy, is Miss Stoner," observed Holmes, shading his eyes. "Yes, I think we had better do as you suggest."

We got off, paid our fare, and the trap rattled back on its way to Leatherhead.

"I thought it as well," said Holmes, as we climbed the stile, "that this fellow should think we had come here as architects, or on some definite business. It may stop his gossip. Good afternoon, Miss Stoner. You see that we have been as good as our word."

Our client of the morning had hurried forward to meet us with a face which spoke her joy. "I have been waiting so eagerly for you," she cried, shaking hands with us warmly. "All has turned out splendidly. Dr. Roylott has gone to town, and it is unlikely that he will be back before evening."

"We have had the pleasure of making the Doctor's acquaintance," said Holmes, and in a few words he sketched out what had occurred. Miss Stoner turned white to the lips as she listened.

"Good heavens!" she cried, "he has followed me, then."

"So it appears."

---

[64] A set of steps that allows humans and not animals to cross over a wall or fence.

"He is so cunning that I never know when I am safe from him. What will he say when he returns?"

"He must guard himself, for he may find that there is someone more cunning than himself upon his track. You must lock yourself from him tonight. If he is violent, we shall take you away to your aunt's at Harrow. Now, we must make the best use of our time, so kindly take us at once to the rooms which we are to examine."

The building was of gray, *lichen-blotched* [65] stone, with a high central portion, and two curving wings, like the claws of a crab, thrown out on each side. In one of these wings the windows were broken, and blocked with wooden boards, while the roof was partly caved in, a picture of ruin. The central portion was in little better repair, but the right-hand block was comparatively modern, and the blinds in the windows, with the blue smoke curling up from the chimneys, showed that this was where the family resided. Some scaffolding had been erected against the end wall, and the stonework had been broken into, but there were no signs of any workmen at the moment of our visit. Holmes walked slowly up and down the ill-trimmed lawn, and examined with deep attention the outsides of the windows.

---

[65] The stone is discolored by a growth of algae bacteria and fungi, the combination of which produces many colors and shapes with different characteristics than its individual organisms.

"This, I take it, belongs to the room in which you used to sleep, the centre one to your sister's, and the one next to the main building to Dr. Roylott's chamber?"

"Exactly so. But I am now sleeping in the middle one."

"Pending the alterations, as I understand. By the way, there does not seem to be any very pressing need for repairs at that end wall."

"There were none. I believe that it was an excuse to move me from my room."

"Ah! that is suggestive. Now, on the other side of this narrow wing runs the corridor from which these three rooms open. There are windows in it, of course?"

"Yes, but very small ones. Too narrow for anyone to pass through."

"As you both locked your doors at night, your rooms were unapproachable from that side. Now, would you have the kindness to go into your room, and to bar your shutters."

Miss Stoner did so, and Holmes, after a careful examination through the open window, endeavoured in every way to force the shutter open, but without success. There was no slit through which a knife could be passed to raise the bar. Then with his *lens* [66] he tested the hinges, but they were of solid iron, built firmly into the

---

[66] The magnifying glass Holmes is famous for using.

massive masonry. "Hum!" said he, scratching his chin in some perplexity, "my theory certainly presents some difficulties. No one could pass these shutters if they were bolted. Well, we shall see if the inside throws any light upon the matter."

A small side-door led into the whitewashed corridor from which the three bedrooms opened. Holmes refused to examine the third chamber, so we passed at once to the second, that in which Miss Stoner was now sleeping, and in which her sister had met her fate. It was a homely little room, with a low ceiling and a gaping fireplace, after the fashion of old country houses. A brown chest of drawers stood in one corner, a narrow *white-counterpaned* [67] bed in another, and a dressing-table on the left-hand side of the window. These articles, with two small wickerwork chairs, made up all the furniture in the room, save for a square of *Wilton carpet* [68] in the centre. The boards round and the panelling of the walls were brown, worm-eaten oak, so old and discoloured that it may have dated from the original building of the house. Holmes drew one of the chairs into a corner and sat silent, while his eyes travelled round and round and up and down, taking in every detail of the apartment.

---

[67] A white bedspread that covered the bed
[68] A type of carpet with a cut pile offering a thick look

"Where does that bell communicate with?" he asked at last, pointing to a thick *bell-rope* [69] which hung down beside the bed, the tassel actually lying upon the pillow.

"It goes to the housekeeper's room."

"It looks newer than the other things?"

"Yes, it was only put there a couple of years ago."

"Your sister asked for it. I suppose?"

"No, I never heard of her using it. We used always to get what we wanted for ourselves."

"Indeed, it seemed unnecessary to put so nice a bell-pull there. You will excuse me for a few minutes while I satisfy myself as to this floor." He threw himself down upon his face with his lens in his hand, and crawled swiftly backwards and forwards, examining minutely the cracks between the boards. Then he did the same with the woodwork with which the chamber was panelled. Finally he walked over to the bed and spent some time in staring at it, and in running his eye up and down the wall. Finally he took the bell-rope in his hand and gave it a brisk tug.

"Why, it's a dummy," he said.

"Won't it ring?"

"No, it is not even attached to a wire. This is very interesting. You can see now that it is fastened to a hook just above where the little

---

[69] A length of rope attached to a bell that could be rung to summon assistance.

opening of the *ventilator* [70] is."

"How very absurd! I never noticed that before."

"Very strange!" muttered Holmes, pulling at the rope. "There are one or two very singular points about this room. For example, what a fool a builder must be to open a ventilator in another room, when, with the same trouble, he might have communicated with the outside air!"

"That is also quite modern," said the lady.

"Done about the same time as the bell-rope?" remarked Holmes.

"Yes, there were several little changes carried out about that time."

"They seem to have been of a most interesting character - dummy bell-ropes, and ventilators which do not ventilate. With your permission, Miss Stoner, we shall now carry our researches into the inner apartment."

Dr. Grimesby Roylott's chamber was larger than that of his stepdaughter, but was as plainly furnished. A *camp bed,* [71] a small wooden shelf full of books, mostly of a technical character, an armchair beside the bed, a plain wooden chair against the wall, a round table, and a large iron safe were the principal things which met the eye.

---

[70] An opening in the wall, often covered with a movable flap, that allows the movement of fresh outside air into a room. It was not necessary to allow air to pass from this bedroom to Roylott's bedroom.

[71] A small portable cot that can be folded.

Holmes walked slowly round and examined each and all of them with the keenest interest.

"What's in here?" he asked, tapping the safe.

"My stepfather's business papers."

"Oh! you have seen inside, then?"

"Only once, some years ago. I remember that it was full of papers."

"There isn't a cat in it, for example?"

"No. What a strange idea!"

"Well, look at this!" He took up a small saucer of milk which stood on the top of it.

"No; we don't keep a cat. But there is a cheetah and a baboon."

"Ah, yes, of course! Well, a cheetah is just a big cat, and yet a saucer of milk does not go very far in satisfying its wants, I daresay. There is one point which I should wish to determine." He squatted down in front of the wooden chair, and examined the seat of it with the greatest attention.

"Thank you. That is quite settled," said he, rising and putting his lens in his pocket. "Hullo! here is something interesting!"

The object which had caught his eye was a small *dog lash* [72] hung on one corner of the bed. The lash, however, was curled upon itself, and tied so as to make a loop of *whipcord.* [73]

"What do you make of that, Watson?"

"It's a common enough lash. But I don't know why it should be tied."

"That is not quite so common, is it? Ah, me! it's a wicked world, and when a clever man turns his

---

[72] A leash that attached to a dog's collar. This one was tied to make a loop that could be tightened.

[73] A tightly twisted flexible cord.

brain to crime it is the worst of all. I think that I have seen enough now, Miss Stoner, and, with your permission, we shall walk out upon the lawn."

I had never seen my friend's face so grim, or his brow so dark, as it was when we turned from the scene of his investigation. We had walked several times up and down the lawn, neither Miss Stoner nor myself liking to break in upon his thoughts, before he roused himself from his *reverie.*[74]

"It is very essential, Miss Stoner." said he, "that you should absolutely follow my advice in every respect."

"I shall most certainly do so."

"The matter is too serious for any hesitation. Your life may depend upon your compliance."

"I assure you that I am in your hands."

"In the first place, both my friend and I must spend the night in your room."

Both Miss Stoner and I gazed at him in astonishment.

"Yes, it must be so. Let me explain. I believe that that is the village inn over there?"

"Yes, that is The Crown."

"Very good. Your windows would be visible from there?"

"Certainly."

---

[74] To daydream or be concentrating on pleasant thoughts.

"You must confine yourself to your room, on pretence of a headache, when your stepfather comes back. Then when you hear him retire for the night, you must open the shutters of your window, undo the *hasp,*[75] put your lamp there as a signal to us, and then *withdraw*[76] with everything which you are likely to want into the room which you used to occupy. I have no doubt that, in spite of the repairs, you could manage there for one night."

"Oh, yes, easily."

"The rest you will leave in our hands."

"But what will you do?"

"We shall spend the night in your room, and we shall investigate the cause of this noise which has disturbed you."

"I believe, Mr. Holmes, that you have already made up your mind," said Miss Stoner, laying her hand upon my companion's sleeve.

"Perhaps I have."

"Then for pity's sake tell me what was the cause of my sister's death."

"I should prefer to have clearer proofs before I speak."

"You can at least tell me whether my own thought is correct, and if she died from some sudden fright."

---

[75] The metal fastener that normally locked the window.
[76] Leave an area or place currently occupied.

"No, I do not think so. I think that there was probably some more tangible cause. And now, Miss Stoner, we must leave you, for if Dr. Roylott returned and saw us, our journey would be in vain. Goodbye, and be brave, for if you will do what I have told you, you may rest assured that we shall soon drive away the dangers that threaten you."

Sherlock Holmes and I had no difficulty in engaging a bedroom and sitting-room at the Crown Inn. They were on the upper floor, and from our window we could command a view of the avenue gate, and of the inhabited wing of Stoke Moran Manor House. At dusk we saw Dr. Grimesby Roylott drive past, his huge form looming up beside the little figure of the lad who drove him. The boy had some slight difficulty in undoing the heavy iron gates, and we heard the hoarse roar of the Doctor's voice and saw the fury with which he shook his clenched fists at him. The trap drove on, and a few minutes later we saw a sudden light spring up among the trees as the lamp was lit in one of the sitting-rooms.

"Do you know, Watson," said Holmes, as we sat together in the gathering darkness, "I have really some *scruples* [77] as to taking you tonight. There is a distinct element of danger."

"Can I be of assistance?"

[77] Feelings of doubt regarding the proper action to be taken.

"Your presence might be invaluable."
"Then I shall certainly come."

"It is very kind of you."

"You speak of danger. You have evidently seen more in these rooms than was visible to me."

"No, but I fancy that I may have deduced a little more. I imagine that you saw all that I did."

"I saw nothing remarkable save the bell-rope, and what purpose that could answer I confess is more than I can imagine."

"You saw the ventilator, too?"

"Yes, but I do not think that it is such a very unusual thing to have a small opening between two rooms. It was so small a rat could hardly pass through."

"I knew that we should find a ventilator before ever we came to Stoke Moran."

"My dear Holmes!"

"Oh, yes, I did. You remember in her statement she said that her sister could smell Dr. Roylott's cigar. Now, of course that suggested at once that there must be a communication between the two rooms. It could only be a small one, or it would have been remarked upon at the Coroner's inquiry. I deduced a ventilator."

"But what harm can there be in that?"

"Well, there is at least a curious coincidence of dates. A ventilator is made, a cord is hung, and a lady who sleeps in the bed dies. Does not that strike you?"

"I cannot as yet see any connection."

"Did you observe anything very peculiar about that bed?"

"No."

"It was clamped to the floor. Did you ever see a bed fastened like that before?"

"I cannot say that I have."

"The lady could not move her bed. It must always be in the same relative position to the ventilator and to the rope - for so we may call it, since it was clearly never meant for a bell-pull."

"Holmes," I cried, "I seem to see dimly what you are hinting at. We are only just in time to prevent some subtle and horrible crime."

"Subtle enough and horrible enough. When a doctor does go wrong he is the first of criminals. He has nerve and he has knowledge. *Palmer and Pritchard* [78] were among the heads of their profession. This man strikes even deeper, but, I think, Watson, that we shall be able to strike deeper still. But we shall have horrors enough before the night is over; for goodness' sake let us have a quiet pipe, and turn our minds for a few hours to something more cheerful."

About nine o'clock the light among the trees was extinguished, and all was dark in the direction of the Manor House. Two hours passed slowly away, and then, suddenly, just at the stroke of eleven, a single bright light shone out right in front of us.

---

[78] Two infamous doctors that were arrested, tried and convicted of murder by poison. Both were hanged for their crimes.

"That is our signal," said Holmes, springing to his feet; "it comes from the middle window."

As we *passed out* [79] he exchanged a few words with the landlord, explaining that we were going on a late visit to an acquaintance, and that it was possible that we might spend the night there. A moment later we were out on the dark road, a chill wind blowing in our faces, and one yellow light twinkling in front of us through the gloom to guide us on our sombre errand.

There was little difficulty in entering the grounds, for unrepaired breaches gaped in the old park wall. Making our way among the trees, we reached the lawn, crossed it, and were about to enter through the window, when out from a clump of laurel bushes there darted what seemed to be a hideous and distorted child, who threw itself on the grass with writhing limbs, and then ran swiftly across the lawn into the darkness.

"My God!" I whispered; "did you see it?"

Holmes was for the moment as startled as I. His hand closed like a vice upon my wrist in his agitation. Then he broke into a low laugh and put his lips to my ear.

"It is a nice household," he murmured. "That is the baboon."

---

[79] To leave a place currently occupied.

I had forgotten the strange pets which the Doctor affected. There was a cheetah, too; perhaps we might find it upon our shoulders at any moment. I confess that I felt easier in my mind when, after following Holmes's example and slipping off my shoes, I found myself inside the bedroom.

My companion noiselessly closed the shutters, moved the lamp onto the table, and cast his eyes round the room. All was as we had seen it in the daytime. Then creeping up to me and *making a trumpet of his hand,*[80] he whispered into my ear again so gently that it was all that I could do to distinguish the words.

"The least sound would be fatal to our plans."

I nodded to show that I had heard.

"We must sit without light. He would see it through the ventilator."

I nodded again.

"Do not go to sleep; your very life may depend upon it. Have your pistol ready in case we should need it. I will sit on the side of the bed, and you in that chair."

I took out my revolver and laid it on the corner of the table.

---

[80] Holmes held his hand to his lips so the thumb and forefinger tips touched, and the rest of the fingers curved as well, which confined the sound that exited the lips and directly delivered the words quietly into Watson's ear.

Holmes had brought up a long thin cane, and this he placed upon the bed beside him. By it he laid the box of matches and the stump of a candle. Then he turned down the lamp, and we were left in darkness.

How shall I ever forget that dreadful vigil? I could not hear a sound, not even the drawing of a breath, and yet I knew that my companion sat open-eyed, within a few feet of me, in the same state of nervous tension in which I was myself. The shutters cut off the least ray of light, and we waited in absolute darkness. From outside came the occasional cry of a night-bird, and once at our very window a long drawn, cat-like whine, which told us that the cheetah was indeed at liberty. Far away we could hear the deep tones of the parish clock, which boomed out every quarter of an hour. How long they seemed, those quarters! Twelve o'clock, and one, and two, and three, and still we sat waiting silently for whatever might befall.

Suddenly there was the momentary gleam of a light up in the direction of the ventilator, which vanished immediately, but was succeeded by a strong smell of burning oil and heated metal. Someone in the next room had lit a *dark lantern.*[81]

---

[81] Also called a bulls-eye lantern, this cylindrical device used a burning candle or oil soaked wick as its source of light, and a thick convex glass lens to focus the light into a beam. A metal shutter limited the light when darkness was preferred.

I heard a gentle sound of movement, and then all was silent once more, though the smell grew stronger. For half an hour I sat with straining ears. Then suddenly another sound became audible - a very gentle, soothing sound, like that of a small jet of steam escaping continually from a kettle. The instant that we heard it, Holmes sprang from the bed, struck a match, and lashed furiously with his cane at the bell-pull.

"You see it, Watson?" he yelled. "You see it?"

But I saw nothing. At the moment when Holmes struck the light I heard a low, clear whistle, but the sudden glare flashing into my weary eyes made it impossible for me to tell what it was at which my friend lashed so savagely. I could, however, see that his face was deadly pale, and filled with horror and loathing.

He had ceased to strike, and was gazing up at the ventilator when suddenly there broke from the silence of the night the most horrible cry to which I have ever listened. It swelled up louder and louder, a hoarse yell of pain and fear and anger all mingled in the one dreadful shriek. They say that away down in the village, and even in the distant parsonage, that cry raised the sleepers from their beds. It struck cold to our hearts, and I stood gazing at Holmes, and he at me, until the last echoes of it had died away into the silence from which it rose.

"What can it mean?" I gasped.

"It means that it is all over," Holmes answered. "And perhaps, after all, it is for the best. Take your pistol, and we shall enter Dr. Roylott's room."

With a grave face he lit the lamp and led the way down the corridor. Twice he struck at the chamber door without any reply from within. Then he turned the handle and entered, I at his heels, with the cocked pistol in my hand.

It was a singular sight which met our eyes. On the table stood a dark lantern with the shutter half open, throwing a brilliant beam of light upon the iron safe, the door of which was ajar. Beside this table, on the wooden chair, sat Dr. Grimesby Roylott, clad in a long gray *dressing-gown*,[82] his bare ankles protruding beneath, and his feet thrust into red heelless *Turkish slippers.*[83] Across his lap lay the short stock with the long lash which we had noticed during the day. His chin was cocked upwards, and his eyes were fixed in a dreadful rigid stare at the corner of the ceiling. Round his brow he had a peculiar yellow band, with brownish speckles, which seemed to be bound tightly round his head. As we entered he made neither sound nor motion.

"The band! the speckled band!" whispered Holmes.

I took a step forward. In an instant his strange headgear began to move, and there reared itself

---

[82] A long loose robe worn around bedtime.
[83] A soft shoe with an upward curving toe but without a heel.

from among his hair the squat diamond-shaped
head and puffed neck of a loathsome serpent.

"It is a *swamp adder!* [84]" cried Holmes - "the deadliest snake in India. He has died within ten seconds of being bitten. *Violence does, in truth, recoil upon the violent, and the schemer falls into the pit which he digs for another.* [85] Let us thrust this creature back into its den, and we can then remove Miss Stoner to some place of shelter, and let the county police know what has happened."

As he spoke he drew the dog whip swiftly from the dead man's lap, and throwing the noose round the reptile's neck, he drew it from its horrid perch, and, carrying it at arm's length, threw it into the iron safe, which he closed upon it.

Such are the true facts of the death of Dr. Grimesby Roylott, of Stoke Moran. It is not necessary that I should prolong a narrative which has already run to too great a length, by telling how we broke the sad news to the terrified girl, how we conveyed her by the morning train to the care of her good aunt at Harrow, of how the slow

---

[84]Many scholars have debated the real nature of this serpent. The Indian cobra, the *Naja naja*, is known to climb, has a diamond shaped head with puffed neck, and does have a rapid acting venom that can cause death in a few minutes. Roylott apparently suffered from some medical condition that caused the poison to react more quickly in him than his earlier victim, Miss Julia Stoner.

[85] The King James Bible seems to be quoted by Holmes, for in the eighth verse of the tenth chapter of Ecclesiastes it reads, "He that diggeth a pit shall fall into it; and whoso breaketh an hedge, a serpent shall bite him." The "pit" is Roylott's scheme of murder, and he "fell" or died by his own plan. It seems apparent that Holmes had this full Bible verse in mind, since Roylott did break through the walls of Stoke Moran unnecessarily, and a snake did bite him.

process of official inquiry came to the conclusion that the Doctor met his fate while indiscreetly playing with a dangerous pet. The little which I had yet to learn of the case was told me by Sherlock Holmes as we travelled back next day.

"I had," said he, "come to an entirely erroneous conclusion, which shows, my dear Watson, how dangerous it always is to reason from insufficient data. The presence of the gipsies, and the use of the word 'band', which was used by the poor girl, no doubt, to explain the appearance which she had caught a hurried glimpse of by the light of her match, were sufficient to put me upon an entirely wrong scent. I can only claim the merit that I instantly reconsidered my position when, however, it became clear to me that whatever danger threatened an occupant of the room could not come either from the window or the door. My attention was speedily drawn, as I have already remarked to you, to this ventilator, and to the bell-rope which hung down to the bed. The discovery that this was a dummy, and that the bed was clamped to the floor, instantly gave rise to the suspicion that the rope was there as a bridge for something passing through the hole, and coming to the bed. The idea of a snake instantly occurred to me, and when I coupled it with my knowledge that the Doctor was furnished with a supply of creatures from India, I felt that I was probably on the right track. The idea of using a form of poison which could not possibly be discovered by any chemical test was just such a one as would occur to a clever and ruthless man who had had an Eastern training. The rapidity with which such a poison would take effect would also, from his point of view, be an advantage. It would be a sharp-eyed coroner indeed who could distinguish the two little dark punctures which would show where the poison fangs had done their work. Then I thought of the whistle. Of course, he must recall the snake before the morning light revealed it to the victim. He had trained it, probably by the *use of the milk* [86] which we saw, to return to him when summoned. He would put it through this ventilator at the hour that he thought best, with the certainty that it would crawl down the rope, and land on the bed. It might or might not bite the occupant, perhaps she might escape every night for a week, but sooner or later she must fall a victim.

"I had come to these conclusions before ever I had entered his room. An inspection of his chair showed me that he had been in the habit of standing on it, which, of course, would be necessary in order that he should reach the ventilator. The sight of the safe, the saucer of milk, and the loop of whipcord were enough to finally dispel any doubts which may have

---

[86] Most snakes do not drink milk unless as a substitute for water.

remained. The metallic clang heard by Miss Stoner was obviously caused by her father hastily closing the door of his safe upon its terrible occupant. Having once made up my mind, you know the steps which I took in order to put the matter to the proof. I heard the creature hiss, as I have no doubt that you did also, and I instantly lit the light and attacked it."

"With the result of driving it through the ventilator."

"And also with the result of causing it to turn upon its master at the other side. Some of the blows of my cane came home, and roused its snakish temper, so that it flew upon the first person it saw. In this way I am no doubt indirectly responsible for Dr. Grimesby Roylott's death, and I cannot say that it is likely to weigh very heavily upon my conscience."

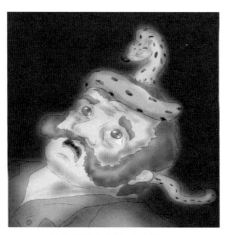

THE END

Appendix A

Another Artistic View

THE ADVENTURE OF
THE SPECKLED BAND

The Original Illustrations That
Accompanied The Adventure As
Published In The February 1892
Edition Of The Strand Magazine

Illustrations By

Sidney Paget

"SHE RAISED HER VEIL."

Illustrations For Pages 6 and 12

"HE HURLED THE BLACKSMITH OVER A PARAPET."

"HER FACE BLANCHED WITH TERROR."

Illustrations For Pages 19 and 29

"WHICH OF YOU IS HOLMES?"

"WE GOT OFF, PAID OUR FARE."

Illustrations For Pages 37 and 45

"WELL, LOOK AT THIS."

"GOOD-BYE, AND BE BRAVE."

Illustration For Page 48

"HOLMES LASHED FURIOUSLY."

Illustrations For Pages 56 and 58

"HE MADE NEITHER SOUND NOR MOTION."

IN COLD BLOOD

A Snaky Suspicion of Michael W. McClure

It is such a pleasant surprise to find that all the greatest Sherlockian chronological scholars of the last century agree upon the date for the "Adventure of the Speckled Band." The good Dr. Watson clearly stated that the investigation took place early in April 1883, and none are so bold as to argue this assignation. To the delight of investigative researchers, such undeniable clarity was not provided for the infamous "murder weapon" used by Dr. Grimesby Roylott.

Of the hundreds of research papers written concerning the "peculiar yellow band, with brownish speckles, which seemed to be bound tightly round (Roylott's) head," there are nearly as many claims as to its possible identity. "It is a swamp adder!" cried Holmes – "the deadliest snake in India." Unfortunately, there is one inarguable problem with his conclusion .... there is no such species listed in the current Reptilia Class. Without a valid hypothesis, researchers have eagerly offered up many alternatives: the puff adder, a Russell's viper, the banded krait of India, the Indian cobra (*Naja naja*), a mongoose, unknown supernatural beasties or hybrid bred creatures, and a variety of other unlikely denizens of the Animalia Kingdom.

Many scholarly papers have echoed certain discrepancies in this cold-blooded killer's specifications, but these do NOT demand exclusion of a serpentine suspect, as some would have you believe. Many snakes DO climb, and snakes WILL drink milk

70

or any liquid if they are thirsty enough. Snakes may not be able to hear, but they DO feel the vibrations in the air and are intelligent enough to be trained. All that needs to be done is to identify a candidate that fits Dr. Watson's descriptions and the deadly toxicity of its venom. There is one snake that seems to fit the profile .... the *Bothrops insularis*, more commonly known as the golden lancerhead of South America. Its venom would be quite deadly, especially for the stressed and aging Dr. Roylott, and its pale yellowish coloring, overlaid with a series of brown dorsal blotches, would certainly fit the descriptions from the case report. Sherlock may have been confused with its country of origin and made the easy inference that the reptile accompanied Roylott when he returned from India, but the evil doctor, a collector of exotic animals, certainly may have acquired the serpent from other lands and trained it as his pet while still stationed in southern Asia. The adder and the viper both have extremely similar heads, as Watson described, "... and there reared itself from among (Roylott's) hair the squat diamond-

shaped head and puffed neck of a loathsome SERPENT." Why do we need to dispute any of this biographer's vivid, eye-witness recollections of Holmes' case? Let us embrace his explicit details as evidence, and add the highly venomous pit viper, the Brazilian golden lancerhead, to the imposing list of suspects for the speckled band of Stoke Moran!

The Adventure of the Speckled Band
Possibly THE Most Produced Sherlock Holmes Short Story Ever!

1892 - First published in the February issue of the *Strand Magazine*

1905 - Retitled "The Spotted Band" in the August issue of *New York World*

1910 - Doyle's play (*The Stoner Case*) based on this story premiers in London
  H. A. Saintsbury - Sherlock Holmes / Claude King – Dr. Watson

ABBREVIATED LIST OF APPEARANCES IN FILM

1912 – Franco-British Film Co., *Le ruban mouchete/The Speckled Band*
  Georges Treville - Sherlock Holmes / There was no Dr. Watson -- 40 minutes

1923 – Stoll Picture Productions, in *The Last Adv. of Sherlock Holmes* series
  Eille Norwood – Holmes / Hubert Willis - Watson -- about 28 minutes

1931 – British and Dominion Studios, Lyn Harding reprises his role as Roylott
  Raymond Massey – Holmes / Athole Stewart – Watson --72 minutes

1944 – Universal Pictures, *Sherlock Holmes and the Spider Woman* (device)
  Basil Rathbone – Holmes / Nigel Bruce – Watson -- 63 minutes

1949 – ZIV Television for NBC Story Theater, *Adventure of the Speckled Band*
  Alan Napier – Holmes / Melville Cooper – Watson – 27 minutes

1964 – BBC-2 Television Service, *Detective* series
  Douglas Wilmer – Holmes / Nigel Stock – Watson –50 minutes

1967 – Westdeutscher Rundfunk, *Das Gefleckte Band* – West Germany
  Erich Schellow – Holmes / Paul Edwin Roth – Watson – 66 minutes

1979 – Telewizja Polska (TVP)
  Geoffrey Whitehead – Holmes / Donald Pickering – Watson – 25 minutes

1979 – USSR entry in *Prilucheniya Sherloka Holmsa i Boctora Vatsona*
  Vasily Livanov – Holmes / Vitaly Solomin – Watson – about 80 minutes

1984 – ITV Network/Granada Television
  Jeremy Brett – Holmes / David Burke – Watson – 52 minutes

1985 – Tokyo Movie Shinsha/RAI, *Sherlock Hound,* まだらのひも anime
  Taichiro Hirokawa – Holmes / Kosei Tomita – Watson – 24 minutes

1999 – DiC Entertainment/Scottish Television, *The Scales of Justice*, anime
  Jason Gray-Stanford – Holmes / John Payne – Watson – 22 minutes

2014 – NHK General TV – Japanese puppetry televised series
  Koichi Yamadera – Holmes / Wataru Takagi – Watson – 20 minutes

ABBREVIATED LIST OF RADIO BROADCASTS

1930 – William Gillette – Sherlock Holmes / Leigh Lovell – Dr. Watson

1931 – Richard Gordon – Sherlock Holmes / Leigh Lovell – Dr. Watson

1933 – Richard Gordon – Sherlock Holmes / Leigh Lovell – Dr. Watson

1936 – Louis Hector – Sherlock Holmes / Harry West – Dr. Watson

1939 – Basil Rathbone – Sherlock Holmes / Nigel Bruce – Dr. Watson

1941 - Basil Rathbone – Sherlock Holmes / Nigel Bruce – Dr. Watson

1943 - Basil Rathbone – Sherlock Holmes / Nigel Bruce – Dr. Watson

1945 - Basil Rathbone – Sherlock Holmes / Nigel Bruce – Dr. Watson

1945 – Sir Cedric Hardwicke – Sherlock Holmes / Finlay Currie – Dr. Watson

1947 – Tom Conway – Sherlock Holmes / Nigel Bruce – Dr. Watson

1948 – John Stanley – Sherlock Holmes / Wendel Holmes – Dr. Watson

1948 – Howard M. Crawford – Sherlock Holmes / Finlay Currie – Dr. Watson

1955 – Sir John Gielgud – Sherlock Holmes / Sir Ralph Richardson – Dr. Watson

1959 – Maurice Teynac – Sherlock Holmes / Pierre Destailles – Dr. Watson

1962 – Carleton Hobbs – Sherlock Holmes / Norman Shelley – Dr. Watson

1968 – Carl Pilo – Sherlock Holmes / Lou Tripani – Dr. Watson

1977 – Kevin McCarthy – Sherlock Holmes / Court Benson – Dr. Watson

1988 – William Gaminara – Sherlock Holmes / Walter Hall – Dr. Watson

1991 – Clive Merrison – Sherlock Holmes / Michael Williams – Dr. Watson

1992 – Edward Petherbridge – Sherlock Holmes / David Peart – Dr. Watson

"We continued our systematic survey ..."
(Quote Taken From *The Adventure of the Priory School*)

Official Surveys' Results: The Favorite Sherlock Holmes Short Stories

1894 - Poll Results (Only 24 Stories Were Published At This Time)
#1 *The Speckled Band*
#2 *Silver Blaze*

1927 - Sir Arthur Conan Doyle's Opinion
#1 *The Speckled Band*
#2 *The Red-Headed League*

1944 – *The Baker Street Journal* Survey Favorites
#1 *The Speckled Band*
#2 *A Scandal In Bohemia*

1959 – The Baker Street Irregulars' Top Choices
#1 *The Speckled Band*
#2 *The Red-Headed League*

1989 – *Sherlock Holmes Journal* Survey Results
#1 *The Speckled Band*
#2 *The Red-Headed League*

1999 – World Wide Survey of Sherlock Holmes Scholars
#1 *The Speckled Band*
#2 *The Red-Headed League*

The results make it clear ... *The Adventure of the Speckled Band*
Is **THE** best loved Sherlock Holmes short story!

One last question ... Do you know why Dr. Grimsby Roylott
gave his scaly serpent milk instead of coffee?
The coffee would have made the snake adderly viper-active!

90832226R00052